Enid

CW00865051

The Secret
Door

...and other stories

Bounty
Books

Published in 2015 by Bounty Books,
a division of Octopus Publishing Group Ltd,
Carmelite House
50 Victoria Embankment,
London EC4Y 0DZ
www.octopusbooks.co.uk

An Hachette UK Company
www.hachette.co.uk
Enid Blyton ® Text copyright © 2011 Chorion Rights Ltd.
Illustrations copyright © 2015 Award Publications Ltd.
Layout copyright © 2015 Octopus Publishing Group Ltd.

Illustrated by Dudley Wynne.

ISBN: 978-0-75372-960-1

A CIP catalogue record for this book is available from the
British Library.

Printed and bound by CPI Group (UK) Ltd, Croydon, CR0 4YY

CONTENTS

The
Secret Door

"We shall be dreadfully bored, staying with Great-Aunt Hannah," said Dick gloomily. "She's nice and kind – but there's absolutely nothing to do at Westroofs."

"What's the house like?" asked Lucy. "You've been there, Dick – Robin and I haven't." "Well, it's awfully old – and rather dark inside – and there's a big room called the library, which is lined from floor to ceiling with the dullest books you ever saw – and at night the ivy taps on the window pane and makes you jump!" said Dick.

"Here we are!" said Robin, peering out of the car window as they swung through a pair of enormous old gates. "My goodness – it *is* an old house. Look at the ivy covering it from roof to ground."

Aunt Hannah was waiting to welcome

them. She was a dear old lady, with snow-white hair, pink cheeks, and a very kind smile.

"Welcome to Westroofs!" she said. "I do so hope you won't find it dull, my dears. But when I heard that your mother was ill, I really thought it would be a kindness to her to have you here for a while."

The three children felt sure that it would be very dull indeed at Westroofs. There were no horses to ride, no dogs to take for a walk, and not even a cat with kittens to play with. Still, if only the weather was fine, they could go for walks and explore the countryside round.

But the weather wasn't fine. When they awoke the next morning the rain was pouring down, and it went on all day long. The children roamed about the house, not daring to play any exciting games in case they disturbed Aunt Hannah, who jumped at any sudden shout or stamping of feet.

Next day it was still raining, and the children felt quite desperate. "I've never been so bored in my life," groaned Dick. "Whatever can we do? Let's

go out in the rain."

But Aunt Hannah was afraid they would get wet and catch cold. "No, don't go out," she said. "Wouldn't you like to go and look at the books in the library? There are some that belonged to my great-grandfather when he lived at Westroofs. Very, very interesting."

The children didn't feel as if Aunt Hannah's great-grandfather's books would be at all interesting, but they were much too polite to say so. They went into the big, dark library and switched on the middle light, for it was a very dull day.

"There must be hundreds and hundreds of books here that nobody ever reads or wants to read," said Dick, looking at the crowded, dusty shelves. "Here's one that I'm sure nobody has ever read – 'History of Edward Lucian, born 1762, in the parish of Elham!' Why, half the pages are still uncut. Poor Edward Lucian!"

"Lucian is our family name. Perhaps he was a great-great-great-ancestor of ours," said Robin. "Look, here's a ladder in this corner. Whatever is it for?"

"To climb up to the topmost shelves I should think, if anyone should ever want

a book from there," said Lucy. "Let's put it up. We'll see what kind of books are kept on the top shelf. Do you suppose there are any storybooks at all?"

"Shouldn't think so," said Robin, putting the ladder up by the shelves of books. "Well, here I go. If I see anything exciting, I'll toss it down."

Up he went. The top shelf was covered with thick grey dust. It flew into the air as Robin pulled out one or two books and made him sneeze. The sneeze made him drop a book, and it almost fell on Lucy's head.

"Look out, idiot!" said Lucy, as the book crashed to the floor. It fell half-open, and something flew out of the pages.

"There! One of the pages has got loose," said Lucy. "I'll put it back in its right place."

But when she picked it up, she saw that it was not a loose page but an old, old letter, written on a half-sheet of paper in curious old-fashioned writing. She could hardly make out a word of what it said. She held it out to Dick.

"Look at this old letter," she said. "All

the s's are shaped like f's. It's impossible to read."

Robin came down the ladder. He too looked at the strange letter. He and Dick began to spell it out slowly.

"'Today – I went through – the Secret Door. I have hid my new top there, and the stick I cut from the hedge. William shall not have them. He knows not the way through – through – the Secret Door. He is not – not – allowed in the Sad – Sad' – what *is* this word? – oh, '*Saddle*'. 'He is not allowed in the Saddle Room, and

knows not the Secret Panel there."

The writing ended at that point. The three children were suddenly seized with a great excitement. They stared at one another, feeling rather breathless.

"It's not a letter – it must be part of a diary or something – kept by someone – a boy – who lived here years and years ago!"

"And he had a brother called William. And William didn't know about a secret panel in the saddle-room, or about a secret door. Golly! Let's go and explore! *We* might find them!"

"Where's the saddle-room? Oh, I know – it's the little room at the side of the house, near where the old stables used to be. And it's got panelling all round the walls, I remember! Quick, let's go!"

Forgetting all about putting the ladder back in its corner, or the book back in its place, the children ran out of the dark library, down long passages, and came to the saddle-room.

It was a low, dark room, set round with squared oak panels. Even now there were two or three old saddles hanging on nails, and a crop lay on a shelf. The rest of the room contained chairs and tables turned out from other rooms. It was plainly a kind of store-room now.

"Now – which would be the secret panel?" said Dick, looking round the walls. "Golly, isn't this exciting? Where shall we try first? Not on that wall, because it's almost covered by that big old picture. Let's try over here by the fireplace."

"How do we look for a secret panel, and what does it do?" asked Lucy. "Do we press or push or what?"

"A secret panel was usually put into a wall of panelling to conceal a cupboard, or some sort of secret way out or in," said Dick. "We must press each one, and jiggle it, and see if

we can make one move."

Dick began to knock round the walls. "Thud, thud, thud."

"I might hear if one panel sounds hollow," he said. "If it did, I'd know it could be the secret one."

But none of them sounded hollow. It was most disappointing. "Perhaps the panel is behind that big picture after all," said Dick. "Let's move it."

But they couldn't. It was much too heavy. They gazed round the little room in despair. Then Dick went to where a saddle hung on a great nail, and took it down. "I haven't tried *this* panel," he said, and knocked on it. It sounded hollow!

"It must be the one!" cried Lucy, and they all pushed at the brown, polished panel, and banged on it. But nothing happened. In desperation Dick caught hold of the big nail and pulled at it.

And then, before their eyes, the panel slid downwards a little, and then sideways, quite soundlessly. Behind it was a dark space. The children stared breathlessly.

"We've found it! We've found the secret panel. What's in the hole?"

Dick sped off for his torch, and soon the children were peering into the hole left by the sliding panel. There didn't seem anything to see at all – just a hole, dark and empty.

"Well – if that isn't disappointing!" said Robin. "Just a hole. And anyway, where's the secret door we read about? There's no door here. Nobody could get through this hole."

Dick put his hand right into the dark hole and groped round. His hand suddenly found what seemed to be a handle or knob of some kind. He pulled it.

Behind the children came a sudden grating noise, then a terrific crash. They all jumped violently, very frightened. They looked round, scared.

"It's that big picture. It fell off the wall," said Dick. "And, gosh – look – there's a space behind it. It's the secret door!"

The children stared in delight. There was an opening in the panelling where the great picture had been, an opening big enough to get through! Where did it lead to?

"When I pulled that knob in the hole here it must have worked something that opened the secret door," said Dick. "And when it opened, the picture had to fall, of course. Oh, it did make me jump!"

A deep sound suddenly boomed through the house. "The gong – it's dinner-time!" said Lucy, with a groan. "Just as we have found this exciting secret door!"

"Better shut it up again," said Dick. "We won't say a word to Aunt Hannah about it until we've explored a bit. We might find family treasure, or something. You never know!"

Visions of glittering jewels, bags of silver and gold, boxes of coins, flashed into the minds of the children. It was very hard to pull at the knob inside the hole and see the secret door shut itself, when they so badly wanted to go through it. They couldn't lift the heavy picture up again, so they left it standing against the wall. Then they went to wash their hands.

Aunt Hannah beamed at them as they

took their places at the table.

"Well," she said, "it has stopped raining at last – and I have arranged a treat for you this afternoon."

The children looked blank. A treat? The only treat they wanted was to go through that secret door! Why had the rain stopped? They didn't want to leave the house now.

"I've telephoned to Farthington – that's our nearest big town, you know," said Aunt Hannah, "and I've got tickets for the circus there, for you. A car is coming at half-past two, and you shall have a late tea at a very nice shop in Farthington that has chocolate eclairs and meringues."

Now, ordinarily this would have been a simply glorious treat, but not today! Still, since everything was all arranged, the children could only say thank you, and go!

"We'll have to explore this evening," said Dick gloomily. "I can hardly wait! What a pity the circus couldn't have been tomorrow."

It was glorious. Aunt Hannah came

too and seemed to enjoy everything very much.

"Now, when we get home, we will have a quiet game of cards together," she said. "I don't want you to get over-excited tonight, after such an exciting afternoon."

So once again exploring had to be put off, and the children played Happy Families and Snap until bedtime. It was terribly disappointing.

Just as Lucy was about to fall asleep in her bed that night, the two boys came cautiously into her room. "Lucy! Are you awake? We're going to go through that secret door now, tonight! We simply can't

wait. Do you want to come, or will you be frightened, because it's night?"

"Of *course* I want to come!" said Lucy, wide awake immediately. "I'll put on my dressing-gown at once. Oh, how super! I never, never thought you'd go tonight!"

Trembling with excitement, Lucy followed the two boys downstairs and along the passages that led to the saddle-room. Dick pulled at the nail that opened the secret panel. It swung aside as before. He put in his hand and pulled at the knob behind. With a grating noise the secret door opened in the panelling nearby, and the children stared into the gaping hole.

Dick shone his torch there. "A short passage, then steps," he said, in excitement. "Come on!"

He climbed through the secret door, and the others followed. The passage was very short, and ended at some narrow, very steep stone steps that led downwards. Dick felt hot with excitement. Where did they lead to?

He went down cautiously, afraid of falling. The others followed. There were fifteen of these steps, then they ended, and another passage came in sight.

"We must be below ground now!" said Dick. "Here's another passage leading away from the house. I do wonder what it used to be for?"

"Oh, most old houses had secret passages or hiding-places," said Robin. "People in olden days often needed to hide their treasure from enemies – or even to hide themselves. Goodness, isn't it dark – and the roof's so low just here that I have to bend my head."

It was very weird, walking along the narrow, musty passage so far underground. It curved about to avoid rocky parts. Then suddenly Dick came to a standstill.

"Blow! There's been a fall here! Look. The roof has fallen in and we can't get by."

The others crowded up to him and looked over his shoulder. "Yes, we *can* get by," said Robin. "We can kick away the rubble at this side, look, and make a way through. It's easy."

They did manage to make their way through and then, covered with dust, they came to a small underground room! An old bench stood at one side, and a crock for water. On a rough shelf was a dust-covered top and a strange curved stick.

The children gazed at them in delight.

"The top and the stick – which that boy of long ago hid from brother William," said Dick, at last. "How weird. He never came to fetch them again."

They stood in silence, looking round the bare little room– and then Robin gave an amazed cry. He bent down and picked up something. "Look," he said, "do look – *a cigarette end*!"

So it was. The others could hardly believe their eyes. "How did it get here? Who has been here? And when?"

As they stood there they suddenly heard a noise. It seemed to come from above their heads. They looked up and saw that the roof seemed to have a hole in it.

And then, even as they looked, the end of a rope appeared, and the rope itself slid through the hole touching Dick on the shoulder. He shut off his torch at once.

"Someone's coming! But what are they doing here? It's almost midnight. They must be up to something!"

"Get back to where that heap of rubble is," whispered Robin. "We can squeeze through again and stay at the other side and listen. Quick!"

With beating hearts the three hurried to the mass of rubble, squeezed through as quietly as they could, and then stood waiting in the dark, listening and peering through the cracks in the rubble that stretched from floor to roof.

Someone slid down the rope. Then a torch flashed on. "Come on, Bill," said a man's voice. "Buck up with the stuff!"

The man took a candle from his pocket, and set it on the wooden bench. He lighted it, and the children saw by its flickering flame that the man in the underground room was thick-set and very short. As he stood there, waiting, something fell through the hole in the roof, and the man caught it deftly. Then another package came, looking like a sack of something, and then another.

A muffled voice sounded down the hole.

"That's all, Shorty. Come on up. We'll fetch it tomorrow."

Shorty hauled himself up the rope, after blowing out the candle. Then there was silence. The children waited for a while, then cautiously made their way back to the underground room again. There were now three sacks there, tied up at the necks.

"They're full of something hard," said Dick, feeling them. "Got a knife on you, Robin?"

Nobody had, because they all wore dressing-gowns. Robin managed to untie one of the sacks. It was full of little jewel boxes. Lucy opened one, and gasped.

Inside was a most beautiful necklace, that glittered brilliantly in the light of the torch. All the other boxes contained jewellery too.

"Looks like the result of a very successful robbery!" said Dick. "What a wonderful place to hide it! I suppose the burglars didn't know there was another way to this room besides that hole in the roof. What shall we do? Drag the sacks back to the house?"

"Oh *yes*," said Lucy. "They will be such a surprise for Aunt Hannah. I'd love to see her face when she sees all these. And it would be too awful to leave them here, in case those men came back and got them!"

So, puffing and panting, the children dragged a sack each through the rubble and up the passage to the stone steps. Up the steps they went, and along to the secret door. They dumped the sacks in the saddle-room, and sat down, panting and excited.

"You go and wake Aunt Hannah, Lucy," said Dick. So she went up to her great-aunt's room and knocked on the door.

"What is it?" came Aunt Hannah's startled voice. "Oh, you, Lucy. Is somebody ill?"

"No. But, Aunt Hannah, do put on your dressing-gown and come down to the saddle-room," begged Lucy.

"To the *saddle*-room – in the middle of the night!" said Aunt Hannah, beginning to think it was all a dream. "Dear, dear – whatever's happening!"

Soon she was down in the saddle-room, astonished to see the sacks there, and even more astonished to see the

secret door.

"Good gracious!" she said. "So you've found that! The door has not been used for ages – and has been forgotten so long that nobody ever knew where it was – except you children, apparently! Well, well, well – now tell me what's been happening."

So they told her – and when they showed her what was in the sacks Aunt Hannah could hardly believe her eyes. She gasped and blinked, and couldn't find a word to say.

"I suppose we'd better ring up the police, hadn't we?" said Dick. "We could hand these to them and tell them about the burglars plan to go to the underground room tomorrow night – and they could catch them beautifully!"

The police were amazed, and very pleased. "Ho – so it was Shorty and Bill, was it?" said the Inspector. "Well, we've been wanting them for a very long time! The stolen goods all belong to the Duchess of Medlington – my word, she'll be glad to have them back! Smart work, children!"

"Well, it was all because of William's brother, really," said Lucy, and the Inspector stared at her in surprise. William's brother? Whatever was the child talking about?

"Now you really must go to bed, children." said Aunt Hannah. "It's two o'clock in the morning. Shocking! No more finding of secret doors and underground rooms and stolen goods tonight, please. Off to bed with you!"

"Well," said Dick, as they got into bed at last, "we thought this would be the dullest place in the world to stay at – but it's given us a most exciting adventure."

So it had – and it was even more exciting when the Inspector telephoned the next night to say that he had got Bill and Shorty all right. "You can't think how astonished they were when they found that their sacks had vanished out of that hole!" chuckled the Inspector. "And they were even more amazed when my men popped down on top of them."

"Wish I'd been there," said Dick. "I say, Aunt Hannah – do you think I might have that long-ago boy's top? It still spins beautifully."

"Of course," said Aunt Hannah. "And Dick can have the walking-stick, cut so many years ago from the hedge. And as for Lucy, she can have this tiny brooch which has been sent to her by the Duchess herself! There you are, Lucy – now none of you will ever forget the adventure of the secret room!"

Sailor Jim's
Telescope

Sailor Jim had a telescope. He put it on a stand down by the sea-wall, and anyone could have a look through it for ten pence.

"We can see the lighthouse as if it was as near as the sea-wall!" said Peter.

"And you can see that bird far out to sea just as if it was flying by your nose!" said Lucy.

"And if I look at that far-off boat I can even see who's in it!" said James. "It's my cousin Harry and his friend Don!"

Sailor Jim liked the children. He gave them a free peep through his telescope every Saturday morning if they could come and tell him that they had had good marks at school.

And one day George came to tell him a very good piece of news indeed. "Sailor Jim – what do you think!" he said. "I've won a scholarship!"

"You don't mean it!" said Sailor Jim. "Well, well, what brains you must have! Now you tell me what you'd like from me for a reward, and you can have it! A sail in my boat? A fishing-trip with me? What would you like to have?"

"Sailor Jim, I suppose you wouldn't lend me your telescope for just one day, would you?" asked George. "My little sister's ill in bed, and she would so love to have your telescope to look through for a little while. She isn't allowed to read. She could look at the birds in the trees, and the sheep far away on the hill – she'd love that!"

"But I wanted to give *you* a reward, not your sister," said Sailor Jim. "Surely you would like to go on a fishing-trip with me, George?"

"Oh, *yes* – better than anything," said George. "But I know how Pat would like your telescope for just one day. She's often said so."

Sailor Jim didn't know what to say. He really didn't want to part with his telescope for a whole day, especially as there were many people visiting his town now – he would lose a lot of money. But still, he had said that George could ask for what he wanted.

"Right," he said at last. "You can take it tomorrow. But be careful of it, won't you?"

George was delighted. How pleased Pat would be! She would feel better at once.

He called for it the next morning and proudly took it off to his sister. She squealed with delight when she saw it and held out her hands. Soon it was propped up on her bed, and she was looking through it.

"The sheep look so big!" she said. "And

now I can see the two little foals properly in the next field. And I can see the rooks pecking up grubs and the shepherd's dog scratching himself. It's like magic! Everything is so near!"

After tea her mother left her by herself with the telescope. George was out in the garden reading. Pat settled down to look through the telescope. She turned it on Mr Land's farm and watched the hens and the ducks there. She turned it on the big field and saw the cows walking through the gate to be milked.

"And now I'll look at that dear little thatched cottage," she said to herself. The cottage was near a privately owned railway line, and steam trains often

went by. Pat could watch the trains with the telescope as well as have a look at the cottage, with its thatched roof and tall hollyhocks.

"It's rather like a fairy-tale cottage," she thought. "I wonder where the old lady is who lives there? Perhaps she is still having her tea indoors. Oh – here comes a train!"

She heard the rumble and then saw the smoke from the steam engine. The train chugged by the cottage, spitting out smoke and a trail of sparks from its funnel.

It soon disappeared. Pat looked at the

cottage through the telescope again. She saw something on the thatched roof. What could it be?

It moved about. Was it a white bird? No – it couldn't be. It grew bigger. It was – yes, it must be – smoke!

"*Smoke!*" said Pat in alarm. "Smoke on the old cottage's thatched roof! A spark from the engine must have blown there – and it's set light to the dry thatch – the straw has caught alight. Oh dear – the cottage will be burnt down!" The little girl raised her voice and shouted: "Mummy! MUMMY! Quick, come here!"

Her mother and George came running up at once. "Look," cried Pat, pointing out of the window. "A spark has set the roof of that cottage on fire. It's burning. Call the fire engine, quick! I saw it through the telescope George brought me."

Mummy flew downstairs to the telephone. She got on to the fire station at once and told them the news.

"Thanks, madam. The old thatched cottage near the railway, you say? We'll be there in three minutes!"

And so they were! Pat watched the whole thing through the telescope in the greatest excitement. The fire engine raced up. The firemen leapt down. A hose was unrolled, and water began to play on the burning thatch. And in the middle of it all an old lady came angrily out of her cottage.

"What are you doing? What is the meaning of this?" she cried. The firemen pointed to the smoking roof where the flames were now almost out.

"Your roof was on fire, missus," said one. "Just got the warning in time."

"Who gave the warning?" said the old lady, astonished.

"A little girl called Pat, who lives up in that house over there," said the fireman, pointing. "She told her mother and her mother telephoned through to us – and here we are!"

"Thank you, thank you," said the old lady. "I must tell my son, and he will go and thank the little girl."

Who do you suppose her son was? *Sailor Jim.* Wasn't that strange? He was so glad to know that his mother's cottage had been saved that he walked

40

up to George's house that evening and asked to see Pat.

"I'd like to see the little girl who noticed that my mother's roof was on fire," he said to Pat's mother. "I want to thank her."

So up he went into Pat's bedroom – and the very first thing he saw there was his own telescope! He stared at it in astonishment.

"How did you get this?" he asked, picking it up.

"George brought it home for just one day for me to look through – my brother George," said Pat. "And it was when I was looking through it after tea that I saw the roof of that cottage smoking. Wasn't it a good thing I had the telescope?"

"It was," said Sailor Jim. "A very good

thing indeed. And what a very, *very* good thing I lent it to George because he won a scholarship!"

"Oh! Are you Sailor Jim?" cried Pat. "George, George, come quickly, here's Sailor Jim!"

George came in and looked astonished to see Sailor Jim. "Have you come for the telescope?" he asked.

"George, it was Sailor Jim's mother's cottage I saw burning through *his* telescope!" cried Pat. "Isn't it strange – just like a house-that-Jack-built story!"

Sailor Jim laughed. "This is the boy who won a scholarship. This is the man who wanted to give him a reward. This is the telescope he lent him. This is the little girl who used it. That's the cottage she saw burning – and here's the man who came to say thank you for saving his mother's home."

"Oh, Sailor Jim – I'm glad your telescope saved your mother," said George. "What a good thing I asked for it!"

"Yes – and I'm giving you something else now," said Sailor Jim. "Another reward! Will you both come out fishing with me as soon as this little lady is better?"

"I'll be better tomorrow. I will! I will!" cried Pat.

"You get better by next Saturday and we'll go," said Sailor Jim. So Pat is going to get well by then, and off they will all go together to catch plenty of fish for Saturday's supper.

It's strange how things happen, isn't it? You simply never know!

Colin is a
Good Policeman

Colin was saving up to buy a pair of skates. He had put all his Christmas money into his money-box and had put his Saturday money there too, and twenty pence that his daddy had given him for sweeping the snow away from the front path.

The money-box was a fat pig with a slit in its back. The money came out of its tummy, for there was a lock there, and when Colin put in the key and undid the lock, a little trap-door opened and the money fell out.

"Next week I shall be able to buy myself a pair of skates!" said Colin one morning, as he counted out his money. "Hurrah! Then I'll be able to go skating with Ned and Bill! That will be great!"

But something horrid happened before

he bought his skates. A burglar came one night, broke into Colin's house, and took his money-box, Mummy's purse, Daddy's lovely field-glasses, some silver from the sideboard, and a beautiful cup that Daddy had won for a golf prize.

Mummy was dreadfully upset. The policeman came and took notes about everything. Daddy told him to be sure and catch the thief if he could, for Mummy had had a lot of money in her purse.

"And I had a lot in my money-box pig," said Colin, almost crying. "I saved it up to buy some skates. Now my money

is all gone. Please do catch the thief, Mr Policeman."

"I'll do my best," said the policeman, shutting his notebook. "Let me see where he got in, please."

The burglar had got in at a small window that led into the larder. The policeman made some more notes, and then went.

The thief was not caught, because the policeman had no idea who it could be. Day after day went by and still there was no news. Colin got more and more impatient.

"Mummy," he said, "won't that thief ever be caught? What about my money-pig? I wanted to buy my skates this week. Can't I get it back?"

"No, dear, not unless the burglar is caught," said Mummy. "And it doesn't seem to me as if he will be, now."

"But, Mummy, he simply *must* be caught, because I want the money for my skates," said Colin in despair.

"Well, dear, unless you catch him yourself, I don't see how you're going to get back your pig," said Mummy, laughing. "The policeman has done his best."

Colin went out into the garden, nearly crying. To think he had lost all his money like that, when he had saved up so hard. It was too bad.

Then he thought again of what Mummy had said – "Unless you catch him yourself, I don't see how you're going to get back your pig."

"If only I *could* find out who it was," thought Colin. "But I don't know how to begin. I don't know if the burglar was tall or short, fat or thin. I don't know

47

anything about him at all." He thought hard for a minute, and then he frowned. "Wait a minute – I *do* know something about him! He must have been very small to get through that tiny window!"

He jumped up and went to the larder window. Certainly it was very tiny. Colin jumped up to the sill – and he noticed that as he jumped he left deep marks in the bed below. And there, beside his own marks, were two other marks, made by someone else!

He jumped down to look at them. They must have been made by the burglar, for the ground was soft, and there had been no rain to wash out any marks since the

robbery. They were deep, too, just as if the man had jumped up to the sill as Colin had done.

The little boy suddenly felt excited. He knew two things about the burglar now – he was small, because the window was very tiny, and he had big feet, because the marks outside in the bed were large. Good!

Colin found his mother's measuring tape and measured the footmarks carefully. Then he measured his father's slippers, and found that the footmarks were even bigger than the slippers. The burglar had bigger feet than Daddy's!

"A small man with very big feet," said Colin to himself. "What else?"

He sat and thought – and then he rubbed his hands together, for he had thought of something else. Mummy had said how strange it was that Micky the dog hadn't barked at the burglar that night, for Micky always barked at strangers.

"Well, if Micky didn't bark, he must have known the man's voice and smell," said Colin to himself. "And if he knew the man, it means that the burglar must have come here often and spoken to Micky and given him tit-bits to make friends with him. I'm getting on! I'm looking for a small man with big feet, someone who comes here fairly often, and who Micky is friendly with."

Colin felt tremendously excited. He went to the window and jumped up to the sill again. He thought he would jump down into the larder and see how much noise he made. So down into the larder he jumped – and as he did so his coat caught on a nail just below the window and tore.

"Bother!" said Colin, and looked

angrily at the nail. And caught on that nail was a piece of brown cloth with a little red line running through it!

"Gosh!" said Colin. "That's not a bit of *my* jacket! The burglar must have caught his jacket on that nail just as I did – and this is a bit of the jacket that he wore then! Oh, I *am* getting on! Yes, I really am. I know the burglar was a small man with big feet, who comes here often, is friendly with Micky, and wears a brown jacket that has a little red pattern running through it!"

The little boy rushed into the garden and thought of all the men who came to the house. Not the milkman – he was tall. Not the butcher – he had small feet. Not the dustman, nor the postman, nor the baker, because Micky wouldn't be friendly with any of them, and barked madly as soon as they appeared.

"What about the window-cleaner?" thought Colin. "No – he only comes once a month and, besides, he is fat. He could never get through into that tiny window."

There was the man who brought the eggs – but Micky hated him. There was the paper-man – it might be him. He was very friendly with Micky, and he was small too. Also he wore a brown jacket!

"I don't remember if he has big feet, though," thought Colin, jumping up, excited. "I must go and see."

The paper-man lived down the road. Colin did hope it wasn't him, because he was a nice man, and always ready for a joke. He was standing at the door of his shop as Colin ran up.

Yes, his jacket was brown, but it had a blue pattern running through it instead of red – and his feet were not even as large as Colin's daddy's feet; so it couldn't be the paper-man. Colin was glad.

And then suddenly the little boy thought of the man who sometimes came to dig in the garden. He was a

bad-tempered little fellow, and Mummy didn't like him. But Daddy said he needed help, and so he gave him a job in the garden whenever he could, and Mummy made him up parcels of bread and cake and fruit.

"We must always help others who are not so well off as we are," Mummy said to Colin, so the little boy had given Walters, the odd-job man, a whole pound out of his own money at Christmas-time. He had emptied his money-pig and chosen the pound himself to give to Walters.

"Could it be Walters?" wondered Colin. "He is quite small enough to creep in at

the window – and I know he has big feet because I heard him grumbling that he couldn't wear Daddy's boots, they were too small. Micky likes him because he throws him bits of his bread. But I simply *can't* remember the jacket he wears."

Now the very next day the odd-job man came again to dig the garden over. But as it was too frosty Daddy said he could chop wood instead. Colin went down the garden to tell him, and to the little boy's excitement he saw that Walters was wearing a brown jacket with a little red pattern in it – and at one side it was torn!

Colin's heart beat fast. So it *was* Walters who had been mean enough to steal from Daddy and Mummy, who had always been so kind to him!

The boy ran into the house as fast as he could and shouted for his father. "Daddy! I want you! I know who the burglar was last week! Oh, do get my money-pig from him and Mummy's purse and your golf-cup!"

"Colin! Whatever do you mean?" said Daddy, astonished.

"Listen, Daddy," said Colin. "I know all

about the burglar. He's small, because he couldn't get in at the larder window if he were big. He has large feet, bigger than yours, because I measured his footmarks in the bed below the window. He's a friend of Micky's, because Micky didn't bark at him – and that means he comes here fairly often – and he wears a brown jacket made of cloth like this!"

He gave his daddy the bit of torn cloth. "I found it caught on the nail just below the larder window," he said. "And, Daddy, the burglar is Walters! He has got a coat on like that this morning, and it's torn!"

Daddy listened, getting more and more astonished. Mummy couldn't believe her ears.

"Why, you're a splendid policeman, Colin," she said.

"Oh, Daddy – I never did like Walters. You were always so kind to him, and now see how he has returned your kindness! What are you going to do?"

"Ring up the police!" said Daddy, and he did. Well, Colin was quite right, for when the policeman went round to Walters' house, the first thing he saw on the mantelpiece was Colin's money-pig! And in a drawer was Mummy's purse, quite empty, and Daddy's field-glasses. The golf-cup was in a cupboard, but the sideboard silver was gone. Walters had sold it.

Colin was so pleased to get back his pig – but, alas, it was empty! The thief had taken all the money out. Colin nearly wept with disappointment. "I shan't get my skates after all!" he said.

But he did. The policemen were glad to have found the burglar, for Walters

had not only robbed Colin's daddy and mummy, but many others besides. And soon, no doubt, he would have taken things from other houses too. The police were glad to have found the thief, for they had been looking for him for a long time – and what do you think they did? They sent to the toy-shop, and they bought a fine pair of skates for Colin!

The little boy opened the parcel, and saw the note with it: "A pair of skates for a good policeman!" and he squealed in delight.

"They are much finer than the ones I had saved up to buy. Oh, I *am* lucky!"

And you should just see him whizzing along on them! Goodness me, he goes as fast as the wind!

Little
Lucky Man

Once Melanie had a tiny little man out of a Christmas cracker. He was so small that he wasn't much taller than a pin!

"Oh, *look*!" cried Melanie in delight, as he fell out on to the table. "A teeny little man – dressed in blue and white – with the tiniest smile on his face!" She held him up. "Look, Mummy, isn't he sweet? I know he's a lucky man!"

Well, it did really seem as if the little man was lucky, because all kinds of things began to happen to Melanie after that. She had invitations to four parties and a pantomime. She found some money she had lost. She was given a big box of chocolates by an uncle who had never given her anything before.

"I'm sure it's this tiny man who's bringing me luck!" said Melanie to John, her brother. "Ever since I've had him nice things have been happening to me. Oh, little lucky man, I shall keep you safe. I should hate to lose you. You might take your good luck away with you!"

"Lend him to me," said John, who had not had very good luck that week. Daddy had smacked him for being cheeky. He had lost a pound Mummy had given him for shopping, and he had broken a jug.

"No. You're so careless," said Melanie, holding the little lucky man tightly. "You'd lose him! You always lose everything, John. You even lost your new ball the day after you had it."

"You're really mean," said John. "You won't even spare me a day's good luck! Well, one day I'll get your little lucky man, and I'll hide him where you can't find him and take him about with me. Then, maybe, all kinds of nice things will happen to me, too!"

"You're not to take him away from me!" cried Melanie. "You'll only lose him. I shall be so upset then."

Well, Melanie simply would *not* lend John her lucky man, and, really,

it wasn't very surprising, because John was certainly a very careless boy. He was always breaking his toys, and had lost his two new handkerchiefs, as well as his ball. But John felt certain that if only Melanie would lend him the lucky man even for a day he might find everything he had lost, and get some more good luck besides.

He grumbled about it to his mother. "I do think Melanie might lend me the lucky man. Then things would go right for me, too. I'd get extra presents, and not lose things or break things."

Mummy laughed. "Oh, good luck doesn't come to Melanie because of her lucky man, though she thinks it does. It comes because she's a careful, thoughtful child, who keeps her things nicely – and it comes because she's generous and kind, so that people want to give her presents. You act the same as Melanie, John, and things will go right for you, too."

Melanie kept her lucky little man on a tiny silver chain round her neck. She only took him off when she washed, and then she was careful not to put him in a place where John could find him. John was cross and sulky about it. He was more and more determined to get that little lucky man if he could!

When his birthday came, he had a lovely surprise. His mother and father gave him a new bicycle! His old one had belonged to his cousin and was very rusty and shabby. When John saw his new bicycle he could hardly believe his eyes!

"Oh, Mummy! Daddy! What a wonderful present! *Thank* you!"

"Keep it nice, John," said Mummy. "It looks so beautiful now."

"Can I ring the bell, John?" asked Melanie. She rang it. "Ting-a-ling!" It made a very loud noise indeed. The bicycle had a basket on the front and a saddle-bag full of tools at the back. It really was a beauty.

John went for rides on it every day. He kept it very clean and bright, because he was so proud of it. Then he ran into another boy's bicycle and scratched some

of the brightness from it.

"Oh dear! What a bit of bad luck!" said John in alarm. "I hope I'm not going to have more bad luck – I'm not a very lucky person, really. Wouldn't it be awful if I smashed up my lovely new bike!"

He was so worried that he went to Melanie again. "Melanie, I believe I'm going to have a bit of bad luck again. *Please* lend me your little lucky man to put in my saddle-bag, so that I don't spoil my new bicycle."

"No," said Melanie. "I never will!"

"Mean thing!" said John and went off sulkily. He wondered what Melanie did with her little lucky man now. She didn't wear it round her neck any more. The

teacher at school had said that no child was to wear necklaces, so Melanie had stopped wearing him except at weekends.

John watched to see what Melanie did with the little lucky man whilst she was at school. He soon found out! She put him into the little teapot belonging to her dolls' tea-set. That was a very good hiding-place indeed. John would never, never have thought of it.

He let Melanie go to school before him one morning, and then ran to the playroom, took out the teapot, and lifted out the little lucky man. He put back the teapot and ran to his bicycle. He must hide that little man somewhere on his

bicycle! Somewhere that Melanie would never find. Then the little man would bring him luck, and his bicycle wouldn't have silly accidents and be spoilt. Where should he hide it?

Not in the saddle-bag. Melanie would certainly look there. Not in the basket. He would be far too easily seen. Where, then?

John had a sudden idea. He unscrewed the top off the bell. He put the tiny little lucky man in the bottom of the bell, and then screwed the top on again. He rang the bell.

"Ting-a-ling-a-ling!" Yes, it was quite all right, even with the little man inside it. Aha! Melanie would never, never find him now. John rode off to school, delighted to think that he would have a little good luck himself because he had got Melanie's lucky man.

Well, it certainly was very odd, but things did go very well for John that morning. He was top in arithmetic, he got full marks for dictation, and he jumped higher than anyone else at gym. He did feel pleased.

When he got home that morning he told his mother all about his good luck. Melanie looked sharply at him. Then she went to the playroom and took out her dolls' teapot. She looked inside. No lucky man there! She ran to John.

"You've taken my lucky man! You horrid, mean boy! Give him back at once. Where is he?"

"Shan't tell you," said John. "I'm going to keep him for one whole day. I'll give him back to you tonight. Surely you can spare him just for one day, you mean girl?"

"I know where he is! Somewhere on your bicycle!" cried Melanie, suddenly guessing. "I'll find him! I'll find him!"

She ran to John's bike. He followed her, feeling quite certain that she would never find the little man. Melanie looked in the basket and in the saddle-bag. John stood by, grinning broadly. Melanie felt very angry indeed. "Well, he won't bring you any luck, so there!" she said, almost crying. "He won't, he won't!"

"He has already – and he'll bring me lots more!" said John. And you know, it was very strange, but that afternoon John kicked three goals at football, found the shoes he had lost at school the term before, and was asked out to a party the next day. What luck!

On the way home he had to call and get some shoes from the mender's for his mother. He put his bicycle against the outside of the shop and went in. He had to wait whilst the shoe-mender looked in the rows of mended shoes for his mother's pair.

And would you believe it – when he got outside again, his bicycle was gone! It simply wasn't there at all. John stared at the place where he had left it, but it was quite empty. He went inside the shop and told the man.

"Well, there, now – what a pity!" said the shoe-mender. "There's a lot of bicycles been stolen this week – two of

them from this very street, too. So your lovely new one has gone, has it? What a bit of bad luck!"

Bad luck? It was *dreadful* luck, the worst possible! He had lost his beautiful new bicycle – and didn't know if he would ever see it again. Those bicycle thieves were so very clever.

John went home slowly and sadly, carrying the shoes. He thought of the little lucky man inside the bell. He had gone too. Melanie would never see him again. Oh dear! It seemed as if he had brought bad luck now instead of good.

Melanie was very upset and angry. "I told you that you would have bad luck if you took away my little lucky man!" she scolded. "It serves you right! Now your bicycle has gone, and I expect my good luck has too."

"Don't be so angry with poor John," said her mother. "He is very unhappy about his new bicycle. Daddy is ringing up the police to tell them."

But the police did not think they could get back the bicycle for John. "You see, sir," they said to Daddy, "these thieves are very, very clever. They'll have painted that bicycle green or red or blue by tonight, taken off the basket and saddle-bag, put on others, and done everything they can to make it look like another bicycle altogether. And even if your boy thinks he can recognise his bicycle under a new coat of paint there's no way of telling it's his."

So John had to use his very shabby one again, and he was sad about it. He tried to make things up with Melanie by giving her his old Lego set, but she was very unhappy about her lucky man.

And then something happened. John rode over to the next village to see a friend of his, and on the way back he saw a bicycle standing with others in a shed. It was padlocked so that it could not be stolen. It was painted a bright green, and had on a lamp, no basket, and a very old saddle-bag. But something about it made John feel absolutely certain that it was his! "I know the look of it! I'm sure it's mine, even though it's green now. Oh dear! How can I possibly know for certain that it's mine?"

He suddenly thought of something. He looked for the bell. Yes, that was still there. Could he unscrew the top and look inside before the owner came out – because the little lucky man might still be there? And if he was, that would prove that the bicycle really was John's!

There was no one about. All the men were working in the factory nearby. John went up to the green bicycle and began to unscrew the top of the bell. His fingers trembled so that he could hardly take it off.

But at last it was off. John looked into the bottom part of the bell – and, yes, the little lucky man *was* there! John stared in the greatest delight. Should he take it out? No, because then he would have no proof that the bicycle was his.

He must go to the police station and tell the police there all about it. They could easily telephone the police in the next village where John's home was and

hear all about how his bicycle was stolen.

So off went John to the police station and was soon pouring out his news. The big, stolid policeman listened carefully and wrote down a lot of notes in his notebook. "Thank you, my boy," he said. "Now come with me and show me which is your bicycle."

So off went John and pointed out his bicycle. He unscrewed the top of the bell and showed the little lucky man inside. The policeman chuckled. "Aha! The thief didn't think of any one popping a little fellow like that inside the bell! Well, well – it was a lucky thing for you that you put him there."

John was told to go home and wait. Nothing could be done till the man came out of the factory and unpadlocked his bicycle. A plain-clothes policeman was going to follow him home and see where he lived and who his friends were.

John rushed home and told his mother and Melanie all about it. Melanie was so thrilled to hear that her little lucky man was inside the bell still that she hugged John like a bear. "Oh, if I get him back I'll forgive you for taking him!" she said. "Oh, John – it was bad luck that your bicycle was stolen, but very *good* luck that the little man helped you to know it was yours!"

Two policemen arrived that evening, one with John's bicycle. "We followed the thief," said one of them. "He didn't go home. He went up on the heath to a deserted hut – and there under a pile of sacks we found three other stolen bicycles he was in the middle of repainting. We've got them all now. We arrested the man, of course. He's a thief we've been looking for for a very long time. Thanks to the sharpness of this boy here we've caught him, and been lucky enough to get back other bicycles for their owners as well!"

Melanie watched whilst John undid the bell. He took out the lucky man and gave him to her. She was so pleased to have him again.

"He *is* lucky!" she said. "I don't care what anyone says! He helped you to get back your bike, John – and he got back three other stolen ones – and gave the police enough good luck to catch the thief. He's a very, very lucky little man!"

Well – he certainly seems to be, doesn't he?

Adventure
in the Afternoon

Ian had a camera. He had had it for his birthday, and he was very pleased with it indeed. It wasn't a new one – it was a very old one, really, that his father had seen in a shop and had bought second-hand.

"New cameras are much too expensive," he told Ian. "And, anyway, it is best to learn on an old one – and this is quite a good one. Here's a little instruction book to go with it – it tells you exactly what to do when you want to take a picture."

Ian was thrilled! A camera! Aha – now he could take his own pictures – and what beauties he would get.

"What are you going to photograph?" said Lisa, his sister. "Will you take me, Ian? I'd like you to take a snap of me."

"Oh *no*," said Ian. "I'm not going to waste my precious films on snapshots of *people*, Lisa. Anybody can do that."

"Well, what are you going to photograph?" said Lisa. "Birds? Animals?"

"No," said Ian. "They won't keep still enough for me. I'm going to take pictures of cars and trains and aeroplanes. I'm going to make my own book of cars, to begin with. I shall photograph every kind of car! It will be great fun watching out for them and photographing them."

"Yes. That should be good fun," said Lisa. "Are you going to take a picture of our car, Ian? If you do, I could sit at the wheel as if I'm driving it. Do let me."

So Ian took his first picture – and it was of his father's own car, a Ford, with Lisa sitting up at the wheel as if she were driving it!

He wandered off, with his camera on a strap round his neck. He felt grand with a camera of his own. But he didn't mean to take the things people usually took. No – he was going to take pictures of the things he was most interested in, and those were cars, planes and trains. Ships, too, when he was by the sea.

For the next week Ian had a fine time. He took a picture of a beautiful Rolls Royce, complete with a very grand chauffeur. He took a picture of a tiny little baby-car with a dog at the back. It had been left there to guard the car, and it barked loudly and fiercely at Ian when he came up with his camera.

"Don't you want your picture taken?" said Ian, and he clicked the camera. "Well – I've taken it! And if you come out on

it with your mouth wide open, barking madly, don't blame *me.*"

When he had finished the whole film his father showed him how to develop each picture. Soon Ian had twelve beautiful pictures of cars to stick into his Car Book. He was very proud and pleased.

"You've really done well with your first film," said his father in surprise.

"Well, I read that little book of instructions carefully first," said Ian, "and did exactly what it said."

"Sensible of you," said his father.

"Most people rush at a new thing – they don't trouble to learn anything about it first, and then they wonder why they get poor results. You deserve your camera, Ian."

Ian went on with his photographing of all kinds of cars. He got Ford Fiestas and Volvos, and Volkswagons and Metros and Rovers and Vauxhalls – in fact, all the cars you see rushing about on the roads each day. I expect you know as many as he did.

He stuck the pictures of them in his book. "I've got nearly every make of

car now," he told his father. "I've got American cars too – and look, that's a French one – and there's another. I haven't got an Italian one yet. There's room for that, if only I can get one. They're lovely cars, aren't they, the Italian ones?"

His father didn't know as much about cars as Ian did, and he laughed. "Funny hobby, this, of yours," he said to Ian. "I don't know that it's much use, really; it's fun for you, of course, but, honestly,

your book looks rather like a catalogue of second-hand cars."

Ian didn't mind. He enjoyed his hobby, and he loved taking his camera out, ready to snap any new or unusual car that he saw. It was fun to snap them and even more fun to develop the film and see what kind of picture he had got.

One afternoon he was sitting by the roadside, waiting for cars to come by. There was a lovely view to be seen from the place he had chosen and cars often pulled up to look at it. Then Ian could snap them if they were cars he wanted.

It was very hot indeed. Ian moved out of the sun and snuggled into the greenery of the hedge. His eyes shut. He was asleep!

He was awakened by the sound of a car pulling up near to him. He opened his eyes, yawned and poked his head out of the shady greenery around. Then he sat up straight in delight.

An Italian car! A real beauty – a big yellow one with bright silver lines shining here and there. What a car! Just what he wanted for his book of car photographs.

He pulled his camera case over to him and took out his camera. He saw a man get out of the car and walk to the wall on the other side of the road. He had something in his hand, but Ian couldn't see what it was.

To the boy's surprise the man lifted his hand and threw what he was holding over the wall. Then he walked back to the car. "They'll be off again in half a jiffy," thought Ian. "I must snap the car at once or I'll miss it. What a beauty! I might never see such a fine Italian car again!"

He hurriedly knelt up on one knee and squinted down at the little camera mirror that told him whether the car was in his picture or not. It was – right in the

middle, shining beautifully in the sun. The man was just walking over to it.

Click! Ian snapped down the little lever that took the picture, and at the same moment the driver revved up his engine – *rrrrr-rrrrrr-rrrr*!

The car shot off at top speed. Nobody had spotted Ian in the shade of the hedge. Nobody had heard the click of his camera. How Ian hoped that his picture would come out well! What a beautiful car to add to the collection in his Car Book!

He was walking home, longing to develop his roll of film and see what the picture of the Italian car was like, when he saw a white car coming along in the distance. Ian saw a sign glowing on it: POLICE

"A police car," he said to himself. "A Sierra, and jolly fast too, I should think. I wish they'd stop, because I've got just one more picture to take on this film – and although I've got plenty of Sierras, I've never had one yet with POLICE showing on it."

Just as if the car had heard his wish it slowed down and stopped beside him! Ian hurriedly took his camera out of his case. Now – he could snap this police car.

But before he could snap the car, a uniformed policeman put his head out of the window. "Hey, Sonny! Seen any cars along here lately?"

"Only one in the last half-hour," said Ian. "I fell asleep in the hedge."

The policeman gave an exclamation of annoyance. "Well, you won't be much help then. What was the car you saw?"

"An Italian car," said Jack. "It stopped just by me, and the noise of the engine woke me up."

"Ha! Good!" said the policeman. "Then you can tell me who was in the car – how many – and what they were like."

"Oh – no – I can't tell you that," said

Ian, trying to think hard. "I didn't notice. I just saw a man get out of the car and throw something over the wall down there – some rubbish, I suppose – and then he got back and the car drove away at once."

"What was the man like?" asked the policeman at once.

"I don't know," said Ian. "I really didn't notice, sir."

"Think of that!" said the policeman in an exasperated voice, turning to another man in the car. "Here's a boy who had a good chance of seeing how many there were in the car, what they were like, and everything – and all he knows is what the car looked like!"

Ian felt hurt at the man's tone. "Well, sir, I know you think I'm jolly stupid," he said. "But actually I was photographing the car for my Car Book – so naturally I didn't bother about the people in it."

Then things happened very quickly!

The three policemen in the car exclaimed loudly, one of them hauled Ian into the car, and another whipped his camera case off his shoulder!

"He may have got just what we want!"
said one of them. "We'll get the snap
developed immediately! Johns, you drop
off at the wall where this youngster says
he saw one of the men throw something
over, and see what you can find. We'll
drive on to the police station and get this
film developed at once."

"But it's *my* film!" began Ian
indignantly. "I always develop my own
films. What's all the excitement about?"

"Well, you deserve to know, seeing that

it is likely you may be going to present us with a photograph of one or two people who are concerned in a robbery of valuable State papers," said the first policeman. "We've an idea who they are, but we've no proof at the moment. All we know is that they drove off in a big Italian car."

Now it was Ian's turn to get excited! Fancy his camera snapping the very car with the robbers in – and maybe the very robbers themselves. Ian remembered the man who had been walking towards the car just when he had snapped it. Surely he would be in the picture?

One of the policemen dropped off at the wall and jumped over it to see what he could find. He hoped to get the case in which the stolen papers had been kept. It would be empty, of course – but there

might be fingerprints on it.

The police car sped on to the big police station in the next town. The film was taken from Ian's camera and was soon being developed in a little darkroom. Ian watched in excitement.

At last one of the policemen gave a whistle and held up the roll of film to the light. "Look here! This is the car – and who's that beside it? It's Lennie Richardson, isn't it? We thought he was in on this. And look, here's a man at the wheel, he's come out plainly – my word, it's Pete Lucien!"

"Is it a good snap?" asked Ian, patiently trying to get a peep of it.

"Fine! Couldn't be better!" said the

93

policeman. "What a bit of luck for us! Got the car *and* the men all in one picture – absolutely positive proof of the thieves concerned. Sonny, you did much better than you knew when you snapped that car!"

Well – what a thrill for Ian! The thieves were caught because of his picture, and in the newspapers the next day was the photograph he had taken of the car and the men!

Ian was so proud that he couldn't stop talking about it.

"Fancy my little old camera taking a picture so valuable as that!" he kept saying. "What a fine picture I've got to put in my Car Book – the best and most

exciting of the lot."

All the newspapers that printed Ian's car picture paid him a fee for it – and to his enormous surprise the boy soon had more money than he had ever had in his life!

"Almost one hundred pounds!" he said. "Well, I know what I'm going to do with it!"

I know too, don't you? He's going to buy a really magnificent camera now, for a Train Book. If ever you meet him, ask him to show you his Car Book – it's really very interesting indeed. *Especially* the last two pictures in the book – a big Italian car, shining in the sun – and a gleaming white car with a word showing clearly – POLICE.

"Isn't He a Coward!"

"You're a coward, Harry!" cried Dick.

"I'm not," said Harry.

"Well, climb up to the top of the school wall and jump down, then," shouted David.

"I don't want to," said Harry. "I might twist my ankle and then I shouldn't be able to play football tomorrow. I don't see any sense in doing a thing like that."

"Coward!" yelled everyone. Dick climbed to the top of the wall and stood there, balancing cleverly. Then he jumped down.

"Easy!" he said proudly to Harry. "Go on. Do it. I dare you to!"

"Dares are silly," said Harry. "You know they are. If everybody did all they were dared to there would be an awful lot of broken arms and legs."

"You're afraid," said Mike scornfully. "You say things like that because you are afraid."

"No I don't," said Harry. "I'm not afraid. I've courage enough to stand here and refuse to do something silly which I could quite well do if I tried, haven't I? You wait till there's some real reason for doing things like that and I'll do them. But not just because you dare me to."

"I dare you to jump into the river on the way home!" yelled Mike. "You won't drown because the river isn't deep enough. You just prove you're not a coward, see, and jump into the river!"

"And get soaked just to show you I'm not a coward!" said Harry.

"Cowardy-cowardy-custard!" yelled all the boys and danced round him in delight. "Harry the coward! Coward Harry!"

Harry was tempted to climb to the top of the wall straightaway and jump down, just to show the boys what he thought of them – but he didn't. He *might* just twist his ankle, because the wall was high – and how silly not to be able to play in the football match just because he wanted to show off in front of the boys. Let them think he was a coward if they wanted to. *He* didn't care!

But he *did* care. He cared dreadfully. He hated it when the boys called after him down the street. He couldn't bear it when his mother heard Dick yelling "Cowardy-cowardy-custard!" after him. He began to wonder if he really was a coward.

"I never have done anything brave," he thought. "I've never rescued anyone from drowning or from a burning house or anything like that. I wonder if I *am* a coward. I do hope I'm not."

One afternoon he took another way home and managed to give the boys the slip. He went down Chestnut Way and walked beside the high wall that ran round Chestnut House. A cross old man lived there, with a crowd of growling dogs. Nobody went into the grounds if they could help it.

Round the corner he came across two people. One was a small girl and she was crying. The other was a big boy, bigger than Harry, from the school at the other end of the town.

"What's the matter?" said Harry to the little girl.

"He's thrown my doll over the wall,"

wept the child. "It was Amelia, my best doll. She'll be broken. She'll be eaten up by dogs."

"What a horrid thing to do!" said Harry to the big boy. The boy put up his fists at once.

"I'll fight you if you talk like that to me!" he said.

Then there came a noise of voices and footsteps, and round the corner came Harry's school-fellows – Dick, Mike, David and the rest.

"Here he is!" cried Dick. "Trying to give us the slip. Here's Harry, old cowardy-custard."

"Shut up," said Harry. "Something's happened. This big lout has thrown this little girl's doll over the wall. I was just going to fight him."

The boys stared at the big boy, who still

had his fists up. They looked at Harry, who was much smaller.

"I'll take him on after you've finished with him, Harry," said Dick.

"So will I," said Mike.

The big boy looked scared. "I'm not fighting the whole lot of you," he said – and, quite suddenly, he turned on his heel and fled away as fast as ever he could down the road.

"What did you want to make him do that for, just as I was going to punish him for teasing this little girl?" said Harry crossly to the boys. "He was bigger than me, I know – but I have learnt boxing and I could have beaten him easily."

The little girl gave a sob. "I don't like boys to fight," she said. "I want my doll."

The boys looked up at the high wall. "It's jolly high," said Mike. "Be difficult to get up – and *I* shouldn't like to jump down the other side. I'd be afraid I couldn't get back."

"And those dogs might come rushing up," said Dick. "And that fierce old man might come along."

The little girl wiped her eyes and looked very miserable. "Goodbye!" she suddenly called to her doll over the wall. "Goodbye, Amelia. I can't get you."

Then she suddenly burst into tears again. Harry put his arm round her.

"Don't cry," he said. "I've got a little sister at home just like you – and I've often rescued her dolls for her. I'll get yours. Don't worry!"

"Oh, *will* you?" cried the little girl, and she smiled up at Harry. "But how can you?"

"You just see!" said Harry. He ran a little way up the road to where a tree leaned over the wall. He was up that tree in a flash.

"What are you going to do?" cried Dick. "You can't jump down the other side, idiot. You'd never get back. And those dogs are always about."

"Well, you come and do it, then," said Harry. But nobody wanted to.

They all stood and watched Harry swing himself on to the top of the wall.

The boy looked down the other side. It was a big jump. Bigger than from the top of the school wall. Suppose he broke his ankle?

Well, he wouldn't. He wasn't going

to disappoint the little girl now that he had said he would get her doll. He swung himself down from the wall and landed on the ground. He fell into the soft earth and gave himself only a slight jolt.

The other boys swarmed up the tree that Harry had climbed, and they sat on the top of the wall to watch him. The boy looked for the doll. Ah, there it was, caught in a bush. He went over to get it.

Suddenly, not far off, he heard a bark. Golly, the dogs were about, then! He snatched at the doll.

But before he could get back to the wall and get the other boys to drag him up, a big dog came running round the bushes. He saw Harry and growled. He bared his big teeth.

The boy began to back towards the wall. The dog growled so fiercely that he stopped. The boys on the wall held their breath. Surely the big dog would not fly at Harry?

"What's happening? Oh, what's happening?" cried the little girl, who was on the path outside the wall. "Is that one of the dogs growling at Harry?"

"There are two dogs now – no, three!" said Dick, and stared down from the wall in horror. "Harry – make a dash for it. We'll help you up. Don't be afraid."

"I'm not afraid," said Harry. "But I

know jolly well if I *do* make a dash for the wall the dogs will be on me. I must try to make friends with them, that's all." He boldly held out his hand palm downwards, to the nearest dog.

"Good dog," he said. "Good dog. Fine fellow."

The dog growled, but not so fiercely as before. Harry still held out his hand, then the dog sniffed at it. "Good dog!" said Harry again. "Fine fellow!"

The dog turned his back on Harry as if he was no longer interested in him. Harry stretched out his hand to the second dog. "Good dog!" he began

again. "I'm a friend. A friend, see? And you're a good dog!"

The dog growled. Then he put back his head and barked loudly. Dick almost fell off the wall in sudden fright.

Harry made a move towards the wall. But the second and third dogs came close to him at once, growling. It was plain that they were not going to allow him to escape. Harry looked at them in despair. He couldn't stay there all day! But what was he to do?

The dogs suddenly pricked up their ears and turned their heads. The boys heard a deep voice calling.

"What's the matter with you, Boris?

107

Why are you barking, Leo? Come here, Scamp, and stop your noise."

"It's the old man," whispered Dick to Mike. "Now poor old Harry's properly caught. Let's go while there's time."

"That would be cowardly," said Mike at once. "We must stay and stick by Harry."

A man came round the bushes. He had thick black hair streaked with silver and shaggy black eyebrows that looked very fierce. He frowned when he saw Harry standing there.

"So you came into my grounds and the dogs found you, did they?" he demanded. "And what were you doing here, I'd like to know? Come after my plums?"

"No, sir," said Harry. "I wouldn't dream of such a thing."

The man looked at him closely. "I've seen you before," he said. "Aren't you the boy that the others call 'Cowardy-cowardy-custard' when you go down the road?"

"Yes, sir," said Harry, going red. "But I'm not a coward."

A clear little voice came over the wall. It was the little girl speaking. "He's

brave! A big boy threw my doll Amelia over your wall – and Harry went to fetch her. He isn't a coward, he's brave. Please don't let your dogs hurt him."

The old man saw the doll under Harry's arm. He saw the row of boys sitting on the wall, looking rather ashamed.

"So," he said to Harry, "you, the boy that the others shout after, are the one that jumps down into the grounds where you know there are dogs, to get a little girl's doll. And the others sit up there in safety. Cowards, all of them! Bah! You're worth a hundred of them. Throw the little girl's doll over to her and come and have tea with me. I've got plenty of things a boy like you would like to see."

"Well, thanks very much, sir – but I'd rather go with the others, if you don't mind," said Harry. "They're not cowards, sir – they've often done things they've dared me to do. I'm not a coward either, but they thought I was."

"Well, you're not, Harry. You're braver than any of us!" shouted down Mike. "And more sensible, too. You only do daring things when there's a real reason for them – we did them just for a silly show-off. We'll never call you coward again!"

"Well said!" cried the old man. "Good boy! I'll tell you what we'll do. Harry can go off with you today, but you can *all* come to tea with me tomorrow – yes, and make friends with my dogs, too. Now, over the wall you go, Harry – and I'll see you all tomorrow!"

And up the wall and over he went, dropping lightly down to the other side.

"Good-bye, sir, and thank you!" Harry called. Then the others dropped down beside him. Mike thumped him on the back.

"Sorry we were such idiots about you, Harry," he said. "Let's be friends."

"'Course I will," said Harry. "You just didn't know, that's all. Hallo, here's the little girl again. Come along, we'll take you and Amelia safely home, and if you ever see that big boy again, you tell him Harry will be after him if he teases you any more!"

Then off they went together, laughing and shouting – but the happiest of them all was Harry. He wasn't a coward – and everybody knew it. Hurrah!

When Mac was
a Shadow

Mac lived in a big town. It took a long time to get away from it and out into the country, so Mac used to go to the park to play.

"But you can't really play games like Red Indians in the park," he said to the others. "I mean – people wouldn't like us wriggling through the bushes, stalking one another. But it would be such fun to do things like that."

"Red Indians are babyish," said Tom, a big boy. "It's more fun to play at shadowing, or something like that."

"What's shadowing?" asked Mac. "It sounds good."

"Well – it's what the police do sometimes when they want to watch someone they suspect of something," said Tom. "They tell a man to follow the person around – act like a shadow – always there, but never noticed."

Mac thought about it. Shadowing could really be done anywhere. It might be fun. He asked Tom another question.

"Do you get into trouble if you shadow people for nothing – just for fun, I mean?"

"Not if you're a good shadower!" said Tom with a laugh. "They wouldn't even know you were there. Why – are you thinking of trying it?"

"I might," said Mac. "I shall think about it. It might make up for not playing Red Indians."

He did think about it, and he felt rather excited. Yes – it *would* be rather fun to pretend to be a policeman in plain clothes, and shadow someone – someone who wouldn't even guess that he, Mac, was behind him, watching where he went and what he did. He could pretend the man was an escaped prisoner or something.

So after tea the next evening Mac slipped out by himself. He went into the town and looked round for someone to shadow. "I'll choose a nasty-looking fellow who *might* be somebody bad," he thought. "And I must be very, very careful that he doesn't spot me. If he does, he's won and I've lost. We'll both be playing a game together, but he won't know he is!"

He wandered along the street, keeping his eyes open for a shifty-looking fellow. But everyone seemed to have a pleasant, kindly face. He stood outside a shop and watched.

Somebody came out of the shop and bumped into Mac. "Oh, sorry," he said. "I didn't see you there."

Mac rubbed his knee, where the man's heavy bag had knocked it. "It's all right," he said, and wondered if he should shadow this man. But he looked so jolly and friendly that Mac felt sure he wasn't anyone bad. So he let the man go and he was soon lost to sight.

Then someone else came by – and Mac decided at once that here was a man to shadow. What a nasty-looking fellow! He looked dirty, his hat was pulled well over his face, a cigarette hung from the side

of his mouth, and he slouched along with his hands in his pockets.

"Of course, he won't really be a bad lot at all," thought Mac, "but he looks one, so I'll shadow him."

The man slouched down the street. Mac slipped out of the doorway he stood in and walked after him. The man walked to the corner and turned it. Then he went into a doorway and stood looking at some books there. Mac slipped into another doorway some way behind him and watched to see what the man would do next. Probably go into the shop and buy a book! But he didn't.

He set off again at a fair pace, and then, just as Mac came to the bookshop where the man had stood, the fellow stopped again and looked hard into another window. Mac slid into the doorway of the bookshop and looked at the shelf of books he had seen the man staring at.

He was very surprised when he saw them. They didn't seem at all the kind of books a man like that would study. They were a set of very expensive nature books.

"Oh, well – maybe he's interested in nature," thought Mac, and slipped out of the doorway as he saw the man walking on again.

It was a curious walk that the man took him – a walk that was interrupted by many starings into shop windows, and standing in doorways, looking out. Mac began to feel puzzled. Surely the man didn't know he was following him?

And then, with quite a shock, Mac noticed what the man was doing. *He* was shadowing someone, too! He was following warily, slipping into doorways when the other man stopped to speak to someone, looking into windows if the other stopped to look at something, too. Mac strained his eyes in the half darkness to try and see what he was like.

"He's carrying a bag," he thought. "Why – it's the man who came out of that shop and bumped into me. His bag felt very heavy when it knocked my knee. Maybe there was money in it – people's wages or something!"

On went the man with the bag – on

went the nasty fellow following him – and on went Mac, following too! But now it didn't seem a game any more.

What was the shadower going to do? Was he going to jump on the man with the bag when he came to a dark place, and knock him down, and steal his bag? Mac felt quite sure something horrid was going to happen.

His heart began to beat fast. What could he do? He couldn't possibly stop the man – but neither could he warn the man with the bag! "I must do something,

I really must," thought Mac desperately.

And then he saw Tom! He beckoned to him urgently.

Tom joined him in surprise. "I say, Tom," began Mac, in rather a breathless voice. "You'll have to help me. I came out to have a game of shadowing someone – like you told me, you know – and I chose that horrid-looking fellow, some way in front there, to follow. Do you see him? Well – I've now discovered that *he's* shadowing someone, too – a man with a bag that I'm sure is full of money."

"Golly!" said Tom. "And he's going to knock him on the head when he comes to a dark spot!"

"Yes, I'm sure he is," said Mac. "So look here, Tom – you rush off now and find a policeman and tell him what is happening. It's no good telling the man with the bag, he might just laugh. The policeman will know what to do."

"Right," said Tom, and darted off up the street, passing the shadower and the man with the bag, too. He was soon out of sight, trying to find a policeman.

The man with the bag now walked steadily on. He met no one because he was now in a more deserted part of the town. He turned down a dark lane.

Immediately the shadower hurried a little and began to close in. Mac hurried, too, his heart thumping. The shadower was now almost up to the first man, and Mac saw him raise his arm. Mac yelled loudly as the man with the bag dodged and fell to the ground. He hung on to his bag, though the shadower was tugging hard at it.

And then Tom appeared with a burly policeman! Oh, what a relief! Mac, Tom and the policeman surrounded the surprised thief. The man on the ground got up and dusted himself down. He was feeling dazed – but he still had his bag of money firmly clutched in his hand.

Things happened quickly after that. The thief was arrested at once, and the policeman asked Tom, Mac and the man with the bag to come along, too.

"Good boy, you," said the policeman to

Tom. "Fetched me along just in the nick of time!"

"Oh, it was Mac here who sent me to find you," said Tom. "He was shadowing the shadower, and guessed what was going to happen."

Everyone was most astonished to hear this, especially the thief. "What? You were behind me all the time?" he growled. "What for?"

"Well – just for a game, actually," said Mac. "And then it suddenly changed from a game to the real thing."

"What a bit of luck for me!" said the man with the bag, who was now quite recovered. He patted Mac on the back. "Funny sort of thing to do, though – follow a man you don't know, just for a game. Are you going to be a policeman or a detective or something when you grow up?"

"Well – I might," said Mac, suddenly thinking that it might be a very good idea.

What a hero Mac was at school the next day! The boys crowded round to hear the story, and even the headmaster congratulated him on his adventure. And nicest of all was the reward that came to him from the man with the bag.

"One hundred pounds!" said Mac, hardly believing his eyes! "Well – no more shadowing for me – I'm going to buy a bike with this and ride out into the country each Saturday – and I'm going to play Red Indians there, and go stalking through the fields and hedges."

"Well, mind you don't stalk a bull, young Mac!" said Tom. "I shan't be there to fetch a policeman for you next time, you know!"

Adventure
for Two

"Coming with me in the car?" called Daddy to Philip and Mary. "I'm just going down to see old Mrs Blakey."

"Oh, is she ill?" said Mary. Her daddy was a doctor and went to see ill people every day.

"No, not ill. She's sprained her ankle, that's all," said Daddy. "I'm just going to have a look at it – and then I rather thought I'd go to the bakery and have one of those chocolate ice-creams of theirs. But you know how I hate eating ice-creams alone."

"Oooh, Daddy! Of course we'll come!" said Philip. He came running out of the playroom with Mary. "You're a great Daddy! You always tell us when you're going ice-creaming!"

They went to get their coats. Their

father went out to get his car. He brought it into the front drive.

Philip and Mary came running out. "I'll go in the front now, and you can be there coming back," said Mary to Philip. In they got, and off went the car. Down the drive, out into the road, and up the hill. Down the hill and round the corner – and there was old Mrs Blakey's house, with its thick yew hedge all round the front garden.

"Now you just look after my car for me whilst I'm in the house," said Daddy, "then I shan't need to lock it up. I always have to if there's nobody in it, because my precious case of medicines might be stolen."

"Oh, yes," said Philip. "And some of them are very poisonous, aren't they?"

Daddy went up the path to the house. The children sat in the car, looking at the thick yew hedge. Mary got out.

"I just want to look at the hedge," she said to Philip. "It's so very, very thick. Why, it's thick enough to get right into the middle of it!"

Philip got out, too. They had always

liked old Mrs Blakey's thick yew hedge. Mary parted the green boughs and looked into the depths of the dark hedge.

"Philip!" she said. "Look! There's a kind of passage going right along the middle of the hedge!"

Philip looked. It did really seem like a passage! The leaves there had dried and fallen off, and the middle of the hedge was empty and bare.

"We could almost go along it," said Philip. "Mary – shall we just get into

it for a minute? I believe if we were in the very middle nobody could possibly see us! What a wonderful hiding-place it would make!"

"Let's hide from Daddy!" said Mary at once. "That *would* be fun! He'd come out and look for us – and we wouldn't be there!"

"And we could say something in a very deep, hollow kind of voice," said Philip. "It would make him jump! Come on, Mary, before he comes out."

It was easy to squeeze into the thick yew hedge. Once in the centre the branches closed firmly round them, and nobody could see them.

"But I've got a fine peep-hole, Mary – have you?" asked Philip. "I can see

Daddy's car through it."

"Yes. I've got a peep-hole, too – between some leaves," said Mary. "Philip – supposing somebody comes by – had we better keep still and quiet?"

"Yes," said Philip. "We can't give our hiding-place away!"

"I can hear someone coming now," said Mary, and she looked through her peep-hole. "It's Jimmy White!"

Jimmy passed by, whistling cheerfully. Philip and Mary giggled. They longed to say "Beware, Jimmy!" in a deep, peculiar voice, but they knew Jimmy well enough to know that he would at once go to look in the hedge for the voice!

"Now there's a woman coming," whispered Philip. "I don't know her."

The woman passed, walking quickly. The children sat quite still in their hiding-place. The passer-by didn't know anyone was so near her!

Nobody came for a little while. Then Philip heard soft footsteps. He peeped out.

"Two men, Mary," he whispered. "Aren't they walking quietly!"

The men came up to the car – but they didn't walk past. They stopped just by it. The children held their breath in case their hiding-place should be discovered.

"No one about," said one man in a very low voice. "Whose car's this? It's got a case inside."

"It's Dr Fenton's car," said the other man in such a low voice that the children could hardly hear him. "That will be his case. There will be valuable drugs in there. Any chance of getting them?"

"Better try now, whilst there's no one to see," said the first man. He wrenched the front door of the car open and put his hand in quickly. In a second he had taken

the case and had shut the door quietly.

Then the two men moved off quickly, walking very softly.

The children had seen all this, and were absolutely thunderstruck. Two robbers! Thieves who had dared to open their father's car and take his case – in full daylight, too! Well, you read of such things in the newspapers – but they never, never happened under your nose like this!

"Mary!" said Philip, finding his tongue at last. "We didn't do a thing. We never even shouted."

"I couldn't," said Mary. "It all happened so quickly. What are we going to do? Daddy's case is gone."

"And we were supposed to be in charge of it," said Philip, horrified at the thought. "Goodness – we were pretty feeble, Mary. If only we'd just given one shout those men would have shot off at once, without even opening the car."

"Yes, but it all happened so *quickly*," said Mary, almost in tears. "I couldn't say a word. I did try, but I couldn't. Let's get out of this hedge and tell Daddy."

At that very moment they heard the front door slam, and their father came briskly down the path.

"Now what about our ice-creams?" he called, as he got to the gate.

Philip and Mary were just climbing out of the hedge. They looked untidy and were covered with little bits and pieces.

They looked so very solemn that their father was surprised.

"I say – did you *have* to climb into that dirty old hedge?" he said, opening his car. Then he stopped and stared. "Good gracious – where's my case gone?"

"Daddy, it's been stolen," said Philip. "Oh, Daddy, it was our fault. We were in the hedge when the men came by and we ..."

"Now begin at the beginning and

tell me everything," said Daddy, seeing at once that something serious had happened. So the two children told him everything: how they had got into the hedge, how people had come by, and the two men had come and talked, and then had stolen the case.

"Did they see you?" asked Daddy. "Did they know you were there?"

"Oh no," said Philip. "But we saw *them* all right. We know exactly what they are like and how they are dressed. If we saw them again we'd know them."

"Very well, then – hop quickly into the car," said Daddy. "I'll go to the police-station and collect a policeman in plain clothes, and we'll drive slowly round and about the streets. Maybe we'll see those men again!"

This was all very exciting indeed. The children got into the car, and Daddy drove off. He went first to the police-station, then quickly told what had happened, and was given an extra passenger – a policeman dressed in ordinary clothes.

"They'll have wrapped up that case of

yours in brown paper by now, sir," said the policeman. "No good looking for the case – have to look for a large brown-paper parcel, or a suitcase big enough to have put your case in. They wouldn't be foolish enough to carry your bag openly for long. Good thing these youngsters of yours noticed what the men were like!"

The car drove slowly down one street and up another. "There are two men," said the policeman suddenly. "Sitting on that seat, sir; look – with a big parcel."

"No – that's not the men," said Philip. "Is it, Mary? Our men had different clothes – one was in a brown suit with a brown tie, and the other was in a green jacket with a black tie."

"Right. Go on again, sir, please," said the policeman. "Ah, wait – what about these men coming round the corner with a case?"

The men had on the right-coloured suits, but they were not a bit like the ones the children had seen.

"No – both those men are small," said

Mary, "and our men are tall. One had a little moustache and the other hadn't. And they both wore hats like Daddy's, and one man had a tiny feather stuck into his hat-band."

"My word – these kids of yours notice a lot, don't they?" said the policeman, most impressed. "They'll be telling us how many toes the men had next!"

The children laughed. They were keeping a very close look-out indeed. They had felt so ashamed of letting those men steal their father's case under their very noses; now they felt they really must catch them and get the case back, or they would never forgive themselves.

Up the hill and down. No men at all. Round the town and back again. Plenty of men, but not the ones they wanted.

"Of course they might have gone into a shop somewhere, or the cinema," said the policeman. "They've had time to get a good way away now, and unless they caught a bus or a train they'll probably be sitting down having tea somewhere – or seeing a film. I'm afraid we'll have to give up finding them this way, sir. I've got all particulars from the children – though I'd like to ask them a few questions – and we'll send out descriptions of the men everywhere."

"Right," said Dr Fenton. "Well, would you like to come along to my house and ask the children what else you want to know?"

Mary spoke up in a very small voice:

"Daddy, I suppose we don't deserve those ice-creams now, do we?"

"Bless us all!" said Daddy. "I'd quite forgotten we were going to have some. Yes, of course we'll have them. Constable, will you join us? You can ask your questions in the bakery."

"Yes, sir. It would be quite a treat," said the policeman, beaming round at the two children. "It's a long time since I was taken to have an ice-cream."

They came to the bakery, and they got out. This time Daddy locked his car well and truly. "Though it's rather like locking the stable door after the horse has gone," he told the children. "Come along."

They went into the tea-room of the bakery, but it was tea-time now and the place was full. "I've a little room upstairs," said the shop-woman. "I think there's a table up there, sir."

So up they went and found the table. A girl came to take their order. Whilst they were waiting for their ice-creams the two children looked round the room. They had never been in this little room before, and they didn't think it was as nice as the big one downstairs. Still, the ice-creams would be just as good!

Mary suddenly trod hard on Philip's toe. Philip looked at her in surprise. Then he looked where she was looking, and he

141

went bright red with excitement.

Sitting huddled together in the darkest corner of the little room were the two men who had stolen their father's case! There was no mistaking them at all – one with a little moustache, one with none; one with a green jacket and black tie, and the other in brown with a brown tie.

And under the table was a very large suitcase! The children looked at one another. They didn't dare to whisper their news in case the men suspected something. So Philip took out his little notebook and pencil and scribbled

something in it. He passed it silently to his father.

"Those are the men over there. Look at the suitcase under the table!" That was what he had written.

His father passed the note to the policeman, who looked casually over at the two men. He in turn scribbled a note very quickly and had it ready for the girl when she came with their ice-creams. His note was short and clear.

"Take this to the police-station," was written on the outside. And inside: *"Send two men to Harrison's Bakery at once. Upstairs. Johns."*

The girl brought their ice-creams, took the note, looked at the outside, seemed very scared, and went out quickly. Two other people finished their tea and went. That left only the two men and the children's table.

The girl came back and slid a note into the policeman's hands. One of the two men called out to her.

"Hey, miss – what times does the bus to Highlands go?"

"Not for fifteen minutes, sir," said the girl.

"Good," thought the children. "The men won't slip out yet."

Two strange men came into the tea-room and sat down silently at the table next to the children's. They nodded to the policeman, who at once got up and went over to the two men.

"I have reason to think that there is stolen property in that case of yours," he said. "Will you open it?"

The men leapt up at once, blustering angrily. One caught up the case. "What cheek!" he said. "Who are you to say things like that! I'll report you to the police."

"I *am* the police," said the policeman

stolidly. "Open that case, please."

The men pushed him aside and went to the door. But the other two policemen were there now. No escape that way!

"Huh! Three of you!" said one of the men in disgust. "All right. Open the case. Though how you know it was us that did the job I don't know. There wasn't anyone to see."

"Walls have ears," said the policeman, opening the case and taking out Dr Fenton's bag from inside. "And hedges have eyes!"

Well, of course, the two men had no idea what he was talking about, but the children knew! They were pleased to see the two men marched off.

"I'm glad you've got your bag back, Daddy," said Mary. "We were silly to let it be stolen. What a good thing we came here for ice-creams!"

"It was," said Daddy. "I say – what about another one each just to celebrate your exciting adventure!"

The Twins
Get in a Fix

The twins were a pair of pickles. They were staying at the seaside, and what a mischievous pair they were! They knocked down other children's sand castles, and took their pails and hid them. They borrowed their shrimping-nets without asking, and they really made the other children very angry.

"Leave our things alone!" they said. "You are most annoying children and we won't play with you if you behave like this."

But the twins took no notice. They always did what they liked.

Now one afternoon the bigger children decided to make an enormous sand castle, the biggest anyone had ever built on the beach. The twins were asked if they would like to help, for such a big

castle needed everyone to dig it. But that was too much like hard work for the twins! "No, thank you," said Jim. "We are going shrimping."

"We think sand castles are babyish," said Suzie. So they went off by themselves – but they couldn't help watching that sand castle growing!

It really *was* an enormous one! It was the kind that uncles and aunts and fathers and mothers build when they all get together and borrow our spades. Kevin and Richard, Harry and John, Sara and Mary, Lucy and Fiona, all helped to dig it. The castle grew and grew, and the moat around it became wider and wider and deeper and deeper.

"Gracious!" said Kevin, stopping for a rest. "I really shouldn't think such a big

castle has ever been built before! We shall need steps to get up to the top!"

So they cut steps to go up to the top of it. It looked very grand indeed. The children were sorry when teatime came and they had to go.

"We'll all come back as soon after tea as we can," said Lucy. "Then we can take turns at sitting on the top when the tide comes in."

So they hurrried home and left the big sand castle.

But, you know, as soon as they had gone those twins ran up to look at it – and they walked up the steps right to the very top!

"Oooh! Isn't it a lovely castle!" said Jim. "Let's call it ours. Let's sit on the top."

"Yes, let's," said Suzie. "The tide's

coming in, and it will be fun to see it filling the moat and swishing all round the castle."

So the twins sat on the top and watched the waves creeping nearer and nearer. How they screamed with joy when one ran into the moat and lapped all round the castle!

Just then the other children came back and they shouted with rage when they saw Jim and Suzie on the top of their beautiful castle.

"Get down! It's ours!" they cried. "You wouldn't help to build it and you shan't share it!"

"Well, we just *shan't* get down!" said Suzie, and she laughed. "And if you try and pull us down we shall kick and knock the castle all to bits. So there!"

"You horrid, nasty children!" said Kevin. "You know quite well that *we* built this castle, and *we* wanted to sit on the top when the tide came in. Get down at once!"

"Shan't! Shan't! Shan't!" sang the twins, and they made rude faces at the others. The children round the castle were very angry, but they couldn't do anything. They were so afraid that Jim and Suzie would spoil their lovely castle if they tried to pull them down.

The waves came higher and higher, and the watching children had to run back up the beach. The tide was getting high. They went back and watched their castle.

"We're the kings of the castle, we're the kings of the castle!" sang the twins, and they waved their hands cheekily.

Now that evening the tide was really very high. Big waves swept up to the enormous castle, and lapped all round it every time. Soon the sea was surrounding it, and the waves galloped beyond the castle and up the beach. The castle seemed quite a long way out in the sea.

The twins suddenly looked behind them – and, good gracious, the shore seemed simply miles away! The other children were playing a game of catch-ball and were no longer watching them. It really seemed as if Jim and Suzie were far away, alone on a crumbling island in the middle of the big sea.

"Oh!" squealed Suzie suddenly, very frightened. "The sea's all round! It's deep, it's deep!"

"The castle is breaking to bits – we'll be in the water!" shouted Jim.

"We'll be drowned, because we can't swim!" yelled Suzie. "Help!"

The other children heard the twins shouting, and they looked towards the castle. "It's breaking up and the twins will fall into the deep sea," said Kevin.

"A jolly good thing!" said Lucy. "Let

them have a fright!"

"Well, we can't let them drown," said Kevin. "Where's our boat?"

It was pulled high up on the beach. Kevin and John dragged it down to the water and got into it. They rowed out to the twins, who were now half in the

water, standing on what was left of the castle. A big wave came and splashed right over them from top to toe. They nearly fell over. Kevin reached them just in time.

"This jolly well serves you right!" he said as he dragged them into the boat. "Now, before we take you back to the shore, do you promise to leave our things alone in the future – or do you want to be dropped in the sea again?"

"We promise!" sobbed the twins. So Kevin and John rowed them to the beach, and they ran home to change their clothes, cold and hungry.

And did they keep their promise? Yes, they did, because, naughty as they were, they knew that to break a promise is a dreadful thing to do. So now they are much nicer, but they will never sit on top of any sand castle they build. I'm not surprised – are you?

Adventure
Up a Tree

"Here's a fine tree to climb," said Alan to John. "Let's try this one. I should think it would rock in the wind like a ship."

"Yes – and it doesn't look *too* difficult to get up," said John. "It's jolly high, Alan. We should be able to see a long way from the top."

"Come on, then," said Alan. "I'll go first. I'm better than you at climbing. You follow the way I go."

So up he went. The tree was an oak – wide-spread and very leafy. It wasn't really very difficult to climb. John followed, and soon the two boys had found a nice broad branch, not far from the top of the tree, where they could sit and eat the sandwiches they had brought.

The wind was strong. It shook the tree, and the boys liked that. "Just like a ship swaying on the sea," said Alan. "I almost expect to hear the splash of the waves!"

The two boys were friends. They loved to go out together and find a hidy-hole of some kind. Today, it was a tree. They liked to take their tea, some chocolate and a book, and have a good read together.

"I've got a new adventure book," said Alan. "I'm in the middle of it. I'll lend it to you afterwards, John – it's really exciting!"

"I like adventure stories too," said John. "But I think I'd rather *have* an

adventure than read about one. I've never had an adventure in my life... I don't believe many people do – do you, Alan?"

"Oh, *yes*," said Alan. "And I'm sure adventures happen suddenly. Why, one might happen to us at *any* moment!"

"Pooh," said John, staring down from the tree at the quiet countryside around. "Whatever do you think could happen to us up here, this quiet afternoooon? Nothing at all!"

"I can't really think of anything," said Alan. "But adventures *do* seem to happen out of nothing – at least, they do in books."

"Is that a bird whistling?" said John, lifting his head to listen. "I've never heard *that* song before!"

It was a flute-like whistle, rather like a blackbird's, and it sounded not very far off. Both boys listened, forgetting their talk about adventures. The whistling stopped, and then began again for a bit.

"I don't believe it's a bird," said John. "I think it's someone down in the wood." As he spoke, the boys could hear twigs cracking and the rustling of leaves as somebody pushed his way through the wood below.

"Ssh!" said Alan. "Whoever it is is coming this way. We don't want them to see us. This is our secret hidy-hole today."

The whistling sounded again, exactly the same. "Sounds like a kind of signal to someone," said John. "Somebody meeting someone, I suppose."

"Be quiet – he's coming under our tree," whispered Alan. Both boys sat

159

as still as mice. Alan was right – the newcomer was now directly under their tree. Then all at once another whistle sounded. Someone else was coming, too.

"Can you see who they are?" asked John, in a whisper. "Are they boys? Do you know them?"

Alan peered down through the branches. All he could see was the top of two heads, and each head wore a cloth cap. Then the boys heard men's voices.

"Where's Jim? He's always late! We'll wait for a few minutes, then leave a note for him."

"Right. He'll have to know what to do, and we've got no way of getting in touch except this meeting-place. What's kept him?"

There was the sound of a match striking and then the smell of cigarette smoke. The men were evidently smoking whilst they waited.

The boys whispered together. "We won't make a sound! The men might be angry if they knew we were over their heads."

"All right. Don't drop your book

on them, or you'll give us away. It's slipping off the branch!"

John caught his book before it fell. The men below smoked on without a word. After ten minutes or so they got up. "I'll scribble a note," said one, and there was the sound of rustling paper. Then there was a silence. One of them was writing.

After that the two men went, and the boys heard their voices in the distance. They looked at one another. "It seems

a bit odd, somehow," said John. "What shall we do? Go down and find the note?"

"Well – the third man might come and catch us," said Alan. "One of us would have to stay up the tree and look out for him, I think."

"You go down, then," said John. "I'll stay up here. I'll whistle if I see or hear him. Buck up."

Alan shinned quickly down the tree. He wondered if he ought to read somebody else's note – there really was something a bit peculiar about all this. The two men hadn't sounded nice men – and why should they have a meeting-place in the wood when they ought to be working?

Alan came to the foot of the tree. He looked about for the note, but there was no sign of one. That meant the men must have hidden it somewhere – in some place where the third man would know where to look for it. Alan began to hunt about.

He lifted up a big stone. Nothing there. He parted the leaves of a bush and looked in the middle. Nothing there, either. He saw a rabbit hole nearby and put his hand down. No – nothing to be found.

"How are you getting on?" called John. "Found it?"

"No," said Alan. "I've looked everywhere. I'll just look round the

tree-trunk – there might be a cranny somewhere."

He was right. There was a crack in the trunk just wide enough for him to put in his hand. He slipped it in and immediately felt paper. He drew it out. It was a single sheet torn from a notebook. Alan read what was on it.

"Bring car to l.c. gates, 3:10 sharp."

That was all there was. What in the world did it mean? What were l.c. gates? And did 3:10 mean afternoon or early morning? Alan didn't know.

A low whistle disturbed him. "Alan! Someone's coming!" came John's guarded voice. Alan thrust the paper back into the trunk of the oak and scrambled up the tree again. The two boys waited in silence for the newcomer.

He came straight to the tree. It must be Jim, then, whoever Jim was – the one the other two had waited for. There was the rustle of paper. Jim had known the hiding-place for it and had drawn it out. There was a moment's silence. Perhaps he was now reading the message. Then there was the rustle of paper again.

After that there was only the sound of footsteps going away and twigs crackling on the ground now and then.

The boys slid down the tree. John asked Alan where he had seen the hidden paper, and put his hand into the crack to feel it. At once he felt paper, and drew out the same little sheet that Alan had seen.

But now a few more words had been added. "O.K. Have arranged for us to go to Big Harry's after."

"I don't like this," said Alan. "I shan't put this note back. I shall keep it. It's odd. I'll ask my father about it tonight."

But he couldn't, because his father came home too late that night, and Alan was in bed and fast asleep. John was awake, wondering if by *any* chance they had nearly had an adventure that afternoon. It had all ended rather tamely, for both boys had had to hurry back because they were late, and had raced through the wood and through the town to their homes.

In the morning Alan's father read the newspaper as usual. He gave an exclamation. "Well – what will happen next? Somebody set the level-crossing gates against the 3:10 train very early this morning – and when it stopped a couple of men got into the guard's van, knocked him over the head, took a mailbag and escaped. No sign of them at all!"

Alan listened, open-mouthed. The 3:10! Why, 3:10 was in that note surely? Did it refer to the train that went over the crossing in the middle of the night?

"'L.c. gates' – level-crossing gates, of course!" thought Alan. "We might have

guessed. I must tell Daddy."

"Daddy," he began, but his father was looking at the clock. "Good gracious, I'm late! I shall miss my train. Goodbye, all of you!"

Alan decided to tell John before he said anything. It was Saturday, so he was free. He did the errands for his mother and then shot off to John's. He found John in a most excited state, for he, too, had seen the papers.

"I say, Alan, that note! That was the

plan made for that robbery!" began John, as soon as he saw Alan. "I've worked it all out. They shut the gates, stopped the train, and two of them knocked out the guard and robbed the van. The third man – the one the others called Jim – brought the car to the gates, so that he might take the bag and the other two men away – to Big Harry's, wherever that might be."

"Yes, I know!" said Alan, just as excited. "Golly – we were in the middle of an adventure and didn't know it. We'll have to go to the police now, John. Thank goodness I've got that note, so they'll believe us."

The police were surprised to see the two boys walking into the police station. "Well, boys, what do you want?" said the constable there.

"We've got something to tell you about the men who robbed the train – the 3:10 last night," said Alan.

"Tell away," said the policeman, getting out his notebook.

"There were three of them," said Alan, "and one is called Jim. They had a car waiting at the gates, and they have all

gone to Big Harry's."

The policeman put down his notebook and stared in amazement at Alan. "How do you know all this?"

"We were up a tree near where they met yesterday," said Alan. "They didn't know we were there. They left a note in the tree and we took it. We thought it was all very odd. I meant to tell my father but I fell asleep before he came home. Here's the note."

The policeman whistled in surprise. He took the note and read it. He called through a door. "Hey, come here. There are two boys who know a lot more about last night's happenings than we do!"

Soon Alan was telling his tale from beginning to end. The policemen listened.

"Go out to the tree with one of these boys and see what you can find," the chief said to one man. "Cigarette ends, perhaps – or footprints."

"There *are* cigarette ends – and a

match too – and footprints, but not very distinct!" said John, wishing he had been sensible enough to pick up the cigarette ends and match for himself. They were clues, of course!

"Could you boys recognise these fellows if you saw them again?" asked the chief.

They shook their heads. "No," said Alan. "We only saw the tops of their heads, you see – we were up the tree. But we saw their caps, of course. They all wore cloth caps."

"Would you know those again?" asked the chief at once.

"Oh, yes," said Alan. "We stared down at them for quite a long time! One had a navy blue cap with a tear in it."

"And one had a tweed cap, awfully dirty," said Jack. "And the third one had a brown cap, rather new, with a big button on the top – brown and flat."

"I want you to stay here for a few minutes," the chief said to Alan. "The other boy can go to the oak tree with this constable and bring back anything they find. Then we will all hop over to Big Harry's. So Big Harry knows about this, does he? Well, well – I often wondered what went on at Big Harry's!"

"What *is* Big Harry's?" asked John.

"Just a place where men can sleep for the night," said the chief. "It's a pity you wouldn't recognise these three again – but if you can spot their caps that will be just as good."

John and the policeman went to the tree and collected two cigarette ends and a match. "They smoke Silk Cut cigarettes, sir," reported the constable, when they got back to the station. "And this is a special kind of match, sir – rather big."

"Right," said the chief. "Good. Now, you two boys, I want you to come with me and do a little cap-spotting. Ready?"

Well, it was a real thrill to go in the big

police car and roar down the road to the next town. Alan and John looked at one another in delight. Whoever would have thought such a thing would happen?

They came to a narrow, rather dirty street. At one end was a tall, ugly building. This was Big Harry's.

The police pushed their way into a dark, dirty hall. Pegs ran all the way down, hung with dirty coats and caps and hats. The chief shone a torch on to them.

"Spot the caps, boys," he said. "That one," said John, pointing to a tweed one. "And that one! That's the brown one with the flat button."

"And here's the navy one," said Alan. "There you are, sir, those are the ones."

"Thanks," said the chief. "Now we'll just find Big Harry and tell him to turn

out all his boarders into the street. He won't know why and we shan't tell him! All we want to see is who takes those three caps. Then we shall know what to do!"

To the two boys' enormous disappointment, they had to go back and wait in the police car. They didn't see Big Harry, frightened and blustering when the police told him to turn out all the men who had slept there the night before. Some were still in bed! However, they were all turned out, and, grumbling and grousing, they went to fetch their coats and caps and hats.

Of course, the three thieves took their own caps – and what a shock for them

when the police arrested them and charged them with the robbery of the night before! One of them was smoking a Silk Cut cigarette, and another had a box of matches on him full of matches exactly like the one found under the tree.

"Well, boys," said the chief, when the two boys were back at the police station, excited and thrilled. "You did well to spot those caps! Made our job very, very easy! Those young men will not be wearing caps for a very long time. And a good thing, too."

The boys said goodbye and left together. "What will our parents say?"

said John. "How do you like adventures, Alan? We were in the middle of one yesterday without knowing it!"

"I like them very much – so long as I'm on the right side," said Alan. "I would rather catch a thief than be one. What cowards they were to attack the guard of the train like that! Gracious, John – let's have another adventure, shall we?"

"We'll look out for one," said John. And they are looking very hard. I do hope they find another soon, don't you?

The Train
that Broke in Half

Benny was a funny little boy. He thought
he couldn't do anything well! He was
always afraid of things, so he was shy and
timid, and hadn't any friends.

"Benny, why don't *you* go in for the
races?" his mother said each summer
when the school sports came. But Benny
shook his head.

"No, I'm not good at running," he said.
"I'd only be last, and look silly, mother."

"Benny, why don't you ask to belong to
the Cub Scouts?" said his father when the
spring came and the Scouts and Cubs put
on their uniforms and went to have some
fun in the fields.

"I'd be no good," said Benny. "I'd never
learn enough. You have to know a lot."

"Well, you could learn, as the others
do," said his father. But no – Benny

wouldn't try. He was afraid of looking silly and of being laughed at.

It was the same with everything. When he went to parties, Benny wouldn't play Musical Chairs because he felt sure he would be the first one out. At Christmas-time he wouldn't pull a cracker because he didn't like the bang.

"But, Benny, you've never pulled a cracker in your life, so how do you know you won't like the bang?" asked his mother. "You may love it, as the other children do. Don't be such a little coward."

Well, that was quite the wrong thing to say to shy Benny. He at once thought he *was* a little coward, so he became more ashamed and shy than ever. He thought that everyone must think him a coward, so he wouldn't play games in case he fell down and cried, and he wouldn't go to any parties at all.

It was dreadful. His mother didn't know what to do with such a funny boy. The other children got tired of asking him to play with them and left him quite alone. So Benny played by himself all day long, and hardly opened his mouth at school. And yet, secretly, Benny longed to have friends and to shout and run and play. Poor Benny!

Now, not far from Benny's house ran a railway line, deep down in a cutting. Benny loved to watch the trains that ran by. He liked to hear them hooting as they raced past. He knew every one of them, and would have liked to wave to the engine-driver, but he was much too shy.

One day he was sitting on the fence, watching the trains, when the long train from the nearest big city came by. It was

a corridor train, so that the carriages were closely joined together for people to walk all up and down the train if they wanted to. Benny liked that sort of train, because he could see the people sitting at the dining-tables and having their dinner, and he could see people standing in the corridors and looking out of the window.

With a loud hoot the train came along, deep down in the cutting. Benny looked at his watch. The train was late, and it was hurrying. Not more than ten minutes behind it would come the next train.

"You'd better hurry!" said Benny to the train. He wouldn't talk to other children, but he often talked to animals and trains and cars. The train hooted and went on.

And than a strange thing happened. The three last carriages of the train

suddenly broke away and got left behind!

Benny stared as if he couldn't believe his eyes! The rest of the train went rushing on, and was soon out of sight. Just those three carriages were left behind. They ran a little way, and then stopped on the line.

"It's broken in half," said Benny to himself. "The train's broken in half! Where's the guard? Will he pop his head out of the guard's van and see what's happened?"

But no guard popped his head out. He couldn't because he was in the other part of the train. He had gone to speak to the ticket-collector who happened to be on

the train – so he didn't know anything about his van being left behind.

Nobody was in the last three carriages at all. They were quite empty. There they stood on the line, looking rather silly.

Benny soon saw that there was nobody in them. He stared and stared – and then had a dreadful thought.

What about the next train that would come rushing along in a few minutes' time? It wouldn't know those carriages were left on the line. Nobody knew but Benny. The signal-man didn't know. The

182

engine-driver wouldn't know – and he would go crashing into them!

"Then there would be an accident," said Benny. "Oh dear! Whatever shall I do?"

For once Benny forgot that he thought himself a poor little coward, no good at anything. He only thought of the people in the train that was soon coming into that deep railway cutting, and would crash into the carriages there. Benny sprang down from the fence. "If I run for all I'm worth I could perhaps get to the signal-box in time, and tell the man to change the signal to red!" thought the little boy. "That would stop it!"

He began to run. Benny hadn't thought he was any good at running at all – but how he ran now! His legs twinkled in and out, and his breath came in big pants. His chest felt as if it would burst, but Benny didn't care. No – he must, he must, he *must* get to that signal-box in time!

It was quite a long way – but at last Benny saw it in the distance. His legs were so tired that they could hardly run, but he made them go on and on until

183

he reached the signal-box. The signal man was leaning out of his box, and he saw Benny.

Now in the ordinary way Benny wouldn't have dared to speak to a signal-man – but now he didn't care what he did. He could hear the train coming!

He turned his head, and there it was, rushing along the line – the train that would crash into the three carriages! Benny tried to shout, but his voice was so full of puffs and pants that he could hardly get his words out.

"Signal-man, change the signal to red!" he panted. "There's some carriages left on the line – broken off the last train!"

The signal-man could hardly understand the breathless boy, but he at once pulled a heavy lever – and to Benny's great delight the signal that had been green for the train to pass by, changed to red – just as the train came rumbling up at a great speed.

The driver saw the signal change to red and he put on his brakes very suddenly. With a long screech the train slowed down and then stopped. Passengers

popped their heads out of the windows to see what was the matter.

Benny got back his breath. He yelled to the signal-man: "The last train broke in half! It left three carriages behind up the line. I only just got there in time to warn you."

"Good for you, young man!" said the signal-man. He ran down from his box and went to the engine-driver. Then the train went slowly on, taking the signal-man too, and soon everyone saw the three

left-behind carriages.

"That was a narrow escape," said the engine-driver, looking pale. "I'd have been right into those carriages if you hadn't put the signal against me."

"It's that boy who saved the train," said the signal-man, looking round for Benny. But Benny was gone! You won't believe it, but all his shyness and fear came back again when he saw so many passengers looking at him. He ran home quickly and went into his bedroom. He was trembling now. He couldn't think how he could have done such a thing!

That teatime his mother was full of the whole affair. "Fancy, Benny," she said, "a boy saved the London train! He saw some carriages left behind on the line, and he tore to the signal-man to tell him – and the next train was saved. Oh, Benny – if only you could do a thing like that! How proud Daddy and I would be of you!"

Benny looked at his mother. He knew how often he had disappointed her because he had been so silly and shy and afraid. Now he had a big surprise in store for her!

"Would you really be proud of me?" he

said. "I'd like that, mother!"

"Oh, Benny, I'd be so proud I'd run out and tell everyone about you!" said his mother. "But you're such a funny little quiet boy – you'd never do anything wonderful, you'd be too scared!"

Just then a knock came at the door – and who should be there but the signal-man! He knew Benny and knew where he lived – and he had come to say a few words to him. And behind him was a crowd of children – the boys and girls of Benny's school, who had already heard about Benny from the signal-man!

"Where's Benny?" said the signal-man. "Ah, there you are! You're a hero, Benny! You saved the train! My goodness, I saw you running to my box, and I've never seen anyone run so fast in my life! Never! You'd win any race if you ran like that. I want to shake hands with you."

And he solemnly shook hands with Benny, whilst Benny's mother and father looked on in the greatest surprise.

"But was it our *Benny* who saved the train?" cried his father. "Good gracious! To think Benny could do that! Benny,

Benny, I'm proud of you! I always thought you were a timid little fellow – but my word, you're a hero!"

His mother hugged him. His father clapped him on the back. The signal-man shook his hand up and down – and in crowded all the boys and girls, yelling, "Benny, Benny! Tell us all about it. Come out, Benny, we want to see you."

And then, all of a sudden, Benny was a hero. He didn't feel a cowardly little

fellow any more. He wasn't afraid of anything. He wanted to shout and run and climb. He was changed from top to toe!

"I didn't know I could do it – but I did!" he kept telling himself. "I was wrong about myself. I was silly and shy just because I thought myself to be silly and shy – but I'm not really. I'm brave and bold – I can run very fast. I can do great things! Oh, I'm glad, I'm glad! Everything

will be different now!"

And so it is – for Benny himself is different, you see. The passengers of the train collected money to give to the boy who saved them, and they bought Benny a fine toy motor-car that he drives down the streets every day. And to hear him come hooting along at a fine pace, you'd never think he was once a poor, shy little fellow who couldn't say boo to a goose!

You never know what you can do until you try!

The Train that Broke in Half